THE MAGIC

THE MAGIC OF HAVENLEA

By

Margaret D. Clark

MARGARET D. CLARK

No portion of this book may be reproduced in any form without permission from the author.

Independently published in association with JV Publishing.
jvpublishing@yahoo.com

Copyright © 2022 Margaret D. Clark.
All rights reserved.

ABOUT THE AUTHOR

I live beside the sea with my family and a very spoilt little rescue dog called Rocky.
My hobbies are reading, writing, swimming, walking in the countryside and travelling, and I love good food and ice cream.

Margaret D. Clark, 2022.

A SECRET HIDING PLACE

Lucy gazed out of her bedroom window. The streetlight cast an orange glow over the orphanage grounds making it look mysterious and eerie.

She was so unhappy. It was five weeks since her parents had been lost during a storm at sea. She wondered how long it would take before they were found. It was almost nine o'clock and past her bedtime when she saw Whiskers, the house cat, creeping about in the garden. He had been locked out again. Lucy put on her warm pink dressing gown and fur-lined slippers and went outside into the chilly night air to let the cat in.

'Whiskers,' she called quietly. The cat hissed and arched his back, warning Lucy they were not alone, before running back inside.

'Is someone there?' she whispered into the darkness.

A frightened little elf showed himself.

'I saw you in the circus!' Lucy said. 'What are you doing here?'

'I've run away.'

'Posters have been put-up-all over town offering a reward for your capture, dead or alive.'

'Oh, dear, oh, dear,' he said. 'Where can I go?' He looked about wildly.

'Come with me, and I'll hide you.'

The elf narrowed his eyes. 'How do I know I can trust you and you won't betray me?'

Lucy folded her arms. 'Look, do you want my help or not?' Her teeth chattered with the cold.

'My life is in your hands.'

'Then come with me,' she whispered.

He followed her into the house.

Just inside the entrance was the cloakroom. Children's coats were hanging in neat little rows, and beneath them were several small-sized sandals all lined up in military fashion. Low voices were heard, and a stream of light filtered out beneath a door at the far end of a wide hallway.

Lucy opened the door to one side, and they both hurried in and quickly shut it behind them before switching on the light. They made their way down a wooden staircase to the cellar. It was filled with all sorts of junk and odd bits of furniture scattered about. Boxes were piled neatly on top of one another. A small dirty window looked out onto an overgrown garden at the far end and beneath it was a small bed with bedding and pillows neatly placed beside it, ready to put on.

'Oooh, this is a secret hidey place,' the little elf whispered in delight.

'No one will find you here.' Lucy stared curiously at the strange little elf she had rescued.

He had a round moon face, green eyes, carroty red hair, and large pointy ears. He was still wearing his circus clothes of bright yellow and little red shoes that curled up at the toes. His clothes were scuffed and dirty.

The little elf returned her stare.

Lucy was eight years old with a mass of curly brown hair, bright blue eyes, and a small button nose.

'Would you mind telling me who you are?' the elf said.

'I'm Lucy Brown.'

He smiled. 'My name is Troy, and I am grateful to

you for saving me.'

She shrugged as if it was nothing. 'What happened to you?' she asked curiously.

'I was a prisoner in the circus.' The colour left his face, and he looked as if he was about to faint.

'Sit here,' she said quickly, grabbing the nearest chair.

The elf sat gratefully. He soon recovered, and the colour returned to his face. 'Do you think I could have a drink of water?' he said.

'Yes, I'll get it.' Lucy ran to the tap in the wall, poured cold fresh water into a plastic beaker, and gave it to him. She watched him drink it down all in one go.

'That's better,' he said, putting the beaker beside him. 'Sorry for that. I don't know what came over me.'

Lucy bit her lip. 'You look awful.'

'I've had a terrible time,' he cried and covered his face with his hands.

'Are you going to tell me what happened?' she said as she dragged another chair to sit beside him, eager to hear what he had to say.

He looked at her. 'I was the star of the circus.'

She smiled at him. 'Mum and Dad took me to the circus, and that's how I knew who you were when I saw you in the garden. I thought you were amazing, and the monkeys doing their tricks were so funny, blowing up coloured balloons and then letting them fly off like rockets.' She giggled. 'It made everyone laugh.'

'Monkeys love to show off in front of an audience,' Troy said.

'Why did you run away?'

'I had just gone into the world of humans to look

around. It was such a lovely day,' he added with a faraway look. 'The sun was shining, birds were singing merrily away, and little rabbits were hopping playfully about in the green fields,' he said but paused and scowled.

'Go on,' she prompted.

'I was captured by the meanies.'

She gasped. 'Who are the meanies?'

'The meanies are loathsome creatures. They like to cause trouble and will do anything for a pot of gold. They knew I was an elf with magic powers. I was locked in a cold dark dungeon in a medieval castle. I was there a long time before I was sold to the circus.'

'Yuk!' she cried, screwing her face up in disgust.

The little elf's mouth turned down.

'How did you escape?'

'It was on a wild and windy night when everyone was busy making the big top more secure to stop it from blowing away. I saw my chance, crept away under cover of darkness, and ran for my life, which is why I ended up in the garden. I was desperate to find a place to hide.'

Lucy grinned. 'It's a good job I saw you, then.'

'I will be forever in your debt for giving me safe refuge and saving my life,' he paused for a moment. 'Now, what about you? Have you a tale to tell?'

'I was brought here to the orphanage when my parents were lost at sea. Their boat capsized during a storm. Everyone is out looking for them and thinks they drowned, but I know they are still alive,' she said. 'Because I feel it here.' She placed a hand over her heart.

Troy looked at her. 'Oh, you must believe what your heart tells you.'

'They are marine biologists,' she added proudly. 'And I want to be a marine biologist too when I grow up.'

'That would be wonderful!'

'I hate it here,' she cried.

He looked at her in horror. 'As bad as that?'

'Yes, it is,' she said quietly. 'All the staff are horrible, the food is awful, and there are bars on all the windows.'

Troy's eyes widened. 'That's terrible.'

Madam Grudge, the matron, ran the orphanage with an iron fist. Everyone disliked her. Even the staff were frightened of her. She was a stout little figure with hairs on her chin and eyes as dark as night. She called all the children in her care her little cherubs, but they all knew she was lying and didn't like children one bit. She couldn't wait for that spoilt little brat, Lucy, to become an orphan when the news was made official that her parents had drowned at sea. She would be treated the same as all the other little orphan brats in her care and made to sleep in dormitories and work for their keep.

'Hatchet face is the housekeeper,' Lucy went on, 'the kids call her that because she always looks angry, as if she could murder someone. Cook is horrible too. She is constantly shouting at us.' Lucy looked down at her feet. 'I like to be alone sometimes and come down here to read.'

'How many children live here?' Troy said.

'There are about thirty of us.'

Troy stamped his foot. 'I'll see this place is shut down and the children are taken care of if it's the last thing I do.'

The hall clock chimed the hour of ten.

Lucy jumped up out of her chair like a frightened rabbit. 'I must go, Hatchet face will be doing her rounds, and if I'm not in bed, I will be in trouble. You can sleep in the little bed with the covers on, and you should be nice and warm,' she added quickly, 'I will come back in the morning and bring you something to eat. And don't worry, your secret is safe with me.'

'I know I can trust you,' he said quietly.

'Night, then.' She left quickly, closing the door behind her, and crept upstairs back to her small, dark, dingy bedroom. As she hadn't been officially declared an orphan yet, she still had her own room, unlike the orphans who slept in dormitories.

Lucy was soon fast asleep in her little bed with Whiskers sleeping at the bottom for company.

Troy went to the little bed, waved his arms gently over it, and said some magic words. Then, the bed covers and pillows came to life and sailed gently onto the bed. Troy was thoughtful as he climbed under the covers. No wonder Lucy was so desperately unhappy. He was deeply saddened at all she had told him and was determined to find a way to help them all.

He soon fell into an exhausted sleep.

THE RUNAWAYS

Lucy made another secret journey to the cellar. Three weeks had quickly passed since she had found Troy hiding in the garden. She had enjoyed his company and would miss him when he left.

'I've brought you something special,' she said with a cheeky grin.

A rat ran past Troy's foot and scampered away as she entered.

She smiled. 'I see you've met my friend, Robo.'

Troy smiled back at her. 'He has told me you often come down here and give him nibbles.'

'Yes, I do,' Lucy said, giving him a small piece of cheese, which Robo quickly ate before scampering into the corner to hide. Lucy emptied the contents of her basket onto the small table. There was a delicious-looking meat pie, jam doughnuts, a thick wedge of chocolate cake, and a carton of fruit squash.

'This is an unexpected treat,' Troy remarked. 'But won't anyone miss it?'

'No, it's cook's day off. She will be late back and won't even notice.'

'Are you sure about that?'

'Yes, I am.'

Troy tucked in.

Lucy sat to one side, biting into an apple as she waited for him to finish. 'Hatchet face locks the kitchen to keep everyone out, and no one gets

anything to eat when she is in charge,' she said.
'This is a horrible place,' Troy said grumpily.

COOK IS ON THE WARPATH

Lucy was passing the kitchen when she heard an argument going on.

'Where's my meat pie and jam doughnuts gone?' the cook cried angrily. 'That is what I would like to know. Someone is stealing food.'

'This simply cannot be allowed to go on,' roared Hatchet face. 'There is a thief in the house! I will organise a search party at once. They won't get away with this.'

Lucy tiptoed away and entered the cellar.

'What's wrong?' Troy said, jumping up from his seat.

'Cook is on the warpath and knows food has gone missing.'

'I knew something was wrong as soon as I saw you.'

'Hatchet face is going to organise a search party,' Lucy said. 'It's not safe here anymore.'

'I must leave at once.'

'Where will you go?'

Troy looked into the distance. 'Home.'

'Where is home?'

'I live in a land far, far away.' He sighed longingly. 'I have missed home and my friends so much.'

'I want to come with you,' she said firmly.

Troy gasped. 'That is not going to happen.'

'Well, I'm not staying here in this horrible place. I'm running away too.'

'B-but where will you go? You can't up and off just like that.'

'I can't stay here. Anyway, what do you care?'

Lucy folded her arms.

'That's not fair,' he said.

'You won't get far dressed like that.'

Troy was still wearing his circus clothes. 'Oh, what am I to do?' he said and looked down at his outfit. 'What am I to do?'

'You will need my help.'

Troy stared at her for a moment and knew she was right. 'You had better come with me, then.' He sighed loudly.

As Troy turned away, Lucy grinned.

'I can see you like getting your own way,' he said over his shoulder. Then he smiled, secretly pleased he would have her company.

'That's settled then,' she said. 'Now let me think. You will need a disguise and a hat to hide your large pointy ears. I will give you mine.'

Troy stared at her open-mouthed.

'Hmm,' she said, looking around and tapping her chin thoughtfully. 'Let us look in the junk box. There might be something in there to fit you. They are full of clean clothes donated to the kids in the orphanage, but Hatchet face sells them at the Christmas market.' She rummaged in the nearest box.

Troy stared at her in amazement as she pulled various items out, looked at them, and then threw them in an untidy pile on the floor. The floor was soon littered with odd items of clothing before she found what she was looking for.

'These should fit you.' She tossed a pair of brown trousers, a button-down jacket, and a pair of brown walking shoes to Troy.

'Try them on,' she said. 'And I'll get my hat.' She quickly left.

She returned to find Troy fully dressed in the new clothes that fit him perfectly.

'How do I look?'

She beamed. 'You could be my little brother.'

'Here, take this.' She passed him a woolly hat which he quickly pulled down to hide his large pointy ears.

Lucy giggled. 'You'll do.'

They both smiled and then burst out laughing.

'We must hide your circus clothes,' Lucy said.

The circus clothes and little red shoes were quickly pushed into one of the boxes and covered with more clothes.

'No one will find them there,' Lucy said with a satisfied look.

At that moment, they heard loud voices coming from outside the door.

They stared at each other. They were about to be caught, and there was no escape.

Robo suddenly appeared beside them. 'I will save you,' he squeaked and ran to the top of the stairs.

The door to the cellar opened as Robo ran out.

Cook and Hatchet face both saw the rat at the same time. Cook screamed at the top of her voice. 'LOOK! THERE'S A RAT!'

They both ran, petrified, yelling at the top of their voices as they ran for their lives. They entered a room along the hallway, and the door slammed shut behind them.

Robo came back to the cellar looking very pleased. 'That was fun,' he said.

Troy and Lucy stared at the brave little rat for a moment, and no one spoke. Then they both fell about laughing.

'That was the funniest thing I have ever seen,'

Lucy said.

Troy turned to Robo. 'You have saved me from being caught, and I thank you from the bottom of my heart.'

'Tush, it was nothing,' the rat said.

And they both agreed he had been very brave.

'We must leave as soon as it gets dark,' Troy whispered.

'I'll go and get my things,' Lucy said and hurried away.

It was the happiest Troy had ever seen her.

*****

After checking that the coast was clear, Lucy and Troy set off as soon as it was dark. They were sneaking through the garden when a voice called out.

'STOP, THIEF!'

They both dived into the shrubbery and heard footsteps as someone ran past them and faded away into the distance. The voices were long gone before they dared make a move.

'Come on, it's this way,' Lucy whispered once the way was clear.

They ran into the trees, slipped through the wide orphanage railings, and out to freedom.

They didn't stop running until they were safely away.

It was a warm summer evening, and they found a sheltered spot beneath a giant oak tree, spending the night hiding there until daylight.

They both woke early to the sound of birdsong.

'I hope you slept well,' Troy said, smiling at Lucy.

'I did,' she said.

'We must get as far away from here as possible,' Troy said. 'A search party will be out looking for us.'

THE LOST PUPPY

Lucy and Troy were walking along briskly when they heard a strange noise. They looked around and saw a little puppy caught up in a fishing net that someone had carelessly left. They hurried to the rescue. The little dog yapped and whined pathetically.

'Quick,' Troy shouted. 'Let's get him out of here before he chokes to death!'

Lucy went down on one knee and spoke softly to the little dog telling him not to be afraid as Troy untangled him.

The puppy seemed to understand they were there to help him and stopped wriggling. He was soon free.

Troy scooped him up in his arms and inspected him for bruises and broken bones. 'No harm done,' he said. 'The clods who left this behind haven't the brains they were born with.' He was furious.

'The first thing we learn at school is not to leave any rubbish behind,' Lucy said. 'We must take it home or put it in the bin.' She tenderly patted the dog. 'He is so sweet.'

'We must take him back where he belongs,' Troy said, smiling as the puppy wagged his tail furiously. 'Woof, woof, woof.'

'He has just said thank you for saving him. His name is Scruff,' Troy said, chuckling.

'Did he really tell you his name?'

'He most certainly did.'

Lucy's mouth dropped open. 'I wish I could understand him,' she said.

'Come on, let's take this little bundle of mischief home.'

'I suppose you know where his home is?'

'I do.'

They hurried along until they came to a farmhouse. A little boy sat on a swing in the garden, looking miserable. Scruff barked wildly and wriggled to get out of Troy's arms. The little boy suddenly looked up and saw Scruff, and his face broke into a big grin as he raced towards them. Troy put Scruff down, and the puppy and the boy ran towards each other.

'Scruff!' Scruff!' the little boy cried.

The puppy leapt into his arms and smothered his face in doggy kisses.

'Oh, Scruff, I've missed you!' he said, hugging him closely.

'Well, there is no doubt he is back where he belongs,' Lucy said, smiling.

Troy grinned. 'That is true love.'

'Thank you for finding Scruff,' the little boy said. 'I thought he was never coming back.'

'He was all tangled up in a fishing net that someone had left there,' Troy explained. 'But he's not hurt,' he added quickly. He smiled at the little boy and saw the dirty tear marks that lined his face. 'I'm Troy, and this is my friend Lucy.'

'My name is Rupert Brown, and I am six years old.

They both smiled at him.

'How long has he been missing?' Lucy asked.

'Since dinner yesterday.'

'You had better keep an eye on Scruff in future,' Troy said, smiling broadly. 'He is still a puppy dog and likes to go exploring.'

'Oh, I will,' the boy said. He turned to leave. 'Scruff will be hungry for his dinner.'

They watched him go with Scruff in his arms and disappear into the farmhouse.

'I love happy endings,' Lucy said.

THE MAGIC WATERFALL

They were deep in the woods when Troy stopped to listen.

'What is it, Troy?' Lucy said.

'I sense danger. The meanies are on our trail.'

They heard a broken twig snapping nearby as if someone had stepped on it.

'Run,' whispered Troy, and they ran.

Once safely away, Troy said, 'We can rest here.' They sat on the soft green grass in the shade of a big old oak tree.

After a while Troy's face lit up. 'Listen to that. If I am not mistaken, that sounds like a waterfall.' He jumped up as if he had been stung.

'What's the matter with you?' Lucy said and stood beside him. 'And what are you getting so excited about?'

'You'll see,' Troy said. 'I have to find the waterfall,' he said as he ran off.

They came to the river and saw a beaver swimming nearby.

'Excuse me,' Troy said to the beaver, 'would you mind telling me what direction the waterfall is, please?'

'It's down river,' the beaver replied pleasantly.

'Thank you,' Troy said before setting off again.

'Wait for me,' Lucy shouted, following him.

'Humans are always in a hurry,' the beaver muttered.

They ran along the riverbank until they came to the waterfall.

Troy pointed to the waterfall. 'Wow! Look at that.

What an amazing sight.'

They stood on the bank of a fast-flowing river staring at a magnificent waterfall cascading down into it.

'We must jump in,' Troy said.

Lucy gasped. 'You are joking.'

'You do not understand. That is a magic waterfall, and behind it lies the entrance to my world.'

'Are you sure about that? she said.

'Of course I am. We can jump in together on the count of three.'

'Oh, this is exciting.' Lucy took a deep breath and gave a quick nod. 'Ready when you are.'

'One, two,' Troy counted slowly, 'three,' he bellowed, and they both took a flying leap into the waterfall.

They landed at the entrance to a cave.

Lucy stared around in wonder as soon as her feet touched the ground. 'I'm not a bit wet.'

'Of course not,' Troy said. It was dark in the cave. 'Come on,' he said and switched on the little torch he always carried.

They followed the beam of light as they hurried along but could see daylight a little way ahead flooding in. They stopped when they saw the shadow of a monster on the wall in front of them. He was blocking their way out.

'We can't get past him,' Lucy whispered.

'Stay out of sight, and I will see who it is,' Troy said quietly. He took a deep breath and approached the monster. 'Are you friend or foe?' His legs had turned to jelly, and his heart beat like a drum.

'That depends on who is asking?' came the reply.

'Would you mind moving so we can get out?'

'Is that my old friend Troy?'

'Yes, it's me and is that you, Prickles?' Troy said.

'Why, of course it's me. Who else would I be?'

'Oh, I'm glad it's only you,' Troy said. 'When I saw your shadow on the wall. I thought you were a huge monster going to gobble us up.'

'Oh, dear,' Prickles the hedgehog said, 'that's not my fault, and where have you been hiding all this time?

Troy sighed. 'It's a long story.'

'Ooh, I love adventure stories.'

'I will come back and tell you all about it when I have more time, I promise.'

'Is there someone else here with you?' Prickles asked.

'Only my friend Lucy,' Troy called to her in the darkness. 'You can come out now, Lucy.' She stepped out of the shadows. 'I want you to meet my old pal, Prickles.'

'Oh, this is a surprise,' Prickles said. 'She's a girl. She has a kind look about her,' he added thoughtfully. 'I am very pleased to meet you, Lucy.'

'Hello, Prickles,' Lucy said, grinning widely at the monster hedgehog. 'I am very pleased to meet you too.'

'I suppose you are going to dash off now?' Prickles said.

'I'm afraid so, but I will be back, and then I will tell you everything,' Troy said.

They said their farewells and stepped into the bright sunlight. Lucy looked around in amazement.

'Oh, this is lovely,' she said, staring at all the beautiful flowers and green fields dotted with playful baby rabbits. Squirrels were scampering about in the branches of giant trees that looked as old as time, and birds sang sweetly. Far away, they could see rivers, streams, and mountains reaching into a clear blue sky.

'It's like something out of a storybook,' Lucy said.

Troy smiled. 'You are in my world now,' he said, and all his worries faded. 'Come on. We still have far to go.'

CHICO AND THE OLD WOMAN

They walked merrily along until they saw a caravan hidden in the trees. Nearby, an old woman sat by the fire, stirring the contents of a large, bubbling saucepan. The smell made them hungry.

She looked up when she heard them coming. 'Hello, dearies,' she said. 'Come and have something to eat. I have made plenty.'

Troy and Lucy hurried over to her. They were hungry, and the delicious smell made their mouths water. The old woman poured the soup out and gave them a bowl each, filled to the brim with tasty-looking broth. They accepted eagerly and said thank you, surprised at her generosity.

'Make yourselves comfortable,' she said, giving them each a spoon as they sat beside her and began to eat.

Their bowls were soon empty.

'That was delicious,' Lucy said.

'It was the best meal I have ever tasted,' Troy said and licked the back of the spoon.

They passed the empty bowls back to her, and she put them on the ground.

'Now, perhaps you can do something for me,' the woman said. 'I want you to meet Chico.' She gave a shrill whistle, and a little monkey suddenly darted out of the caravan and jumped onto her shoulder.

'This is Chico,' she said, patting the animal's head. 'You see, dearies, my health isn't good, and I'm getting on in years,' she added softly. 'Since my husband died, I've been alone, and now I've been offered a home with my daughter, but she hasn't room for my little Chico, and I want you to have him.'

'Oh, isn't he adorable,' Lucy said. 'We will look after him.'

Troy smiled. 'He will be safe with us.'

The old lady looked at them. 'He has been a good friend to me all these years, and I want you to look after him until he doesn't need to be with you anymore.'

Troy nodded. 'Understood.'

'You are going on a long journey over the water,' the old woman said with a faraway look in her eyes. 'Look after the little lady,' she warned, pointing to Lucy. 'Danger lies ahead.' She took off a long gold chain from around her neck with a gold medallion attached to it. 'Take this, and it will protect you on your journey.'

She passed the medallion to Troy, and he gazed at it admiringly. He touched the strange markings on it and knew it was a precious heirloom and would protect them from harm.

'It belonged to my husband.'

'Thank you,' Troy said and placed it around his neck, tucking it well into his clothing so it would not be seen. 'I will treasure it always.'

The woman turned to Chico and touched his face. 'I will always love you,' she said, 'but we must part now and say goodbye. They will be kind to you.' She passed the little monkey into Lucy's willing arms.

'Hello, Chico,' Lucy said softly. 'We will look after you now.' The little monkey was content to be held in her arms as if he understood that Lucy was his new mistress.

They turned to leave.

'Bye, bye, dearies,' the old woman called out.

A MAD BULL

It was getting dark when Troy and Lucy saw a barn alone in the middle of a field.

'We can sleep in there tonight,' Troy said.

Chico disappeared into the woods.

'Where's he off to?' Lucy said, watching him as he left.

'He wants to stay out in the fresh air.'

'Well, I don't,' Lucy said. 'Come on.'

They hurried to the barn, opened the door easily, and stepped inside the entrance.

'I DON'T REMEMBER INVITING YOU IN,' came a roar from inside, and a huge bull stepped forward.

Troy stood fearlessly before him. 'There is no need to be rude. We only want shelter for the night.'

Lucy stepped back and peeped over Troy's shoulder.

The big black bull stamped his foot on the ground. 'Just for one night, you say?'

'Yes, please,' Troy said.

'Well, I suppose I can put up with that,' the bull said.

'Thank you,' Troy said, closing the door behind them. 'We are grateful to you for allowing us in.'

They both stared up at the big black bull illuminated by the light of the silvery moon that shone through a hole in the old barn's roof.

'I'm Troy, and this is my friend Lucy.'

'How do you do,' the bull said. 'I am known as Billy Bull. Now, if you will excuse me, I would like to go back to sleep. And you must leave early. If farmer Giles catches you here, he will shoot you.'

Troy gasped. 'Thank you for the warning. We'll leave as soon as it's light.'

'I just hope you don't snore,' Billy said, giving a loud snort.

Troy looked around at the straw scattered about. 'We can sleep here,' he said, going over to the straw at the back of the barn. 'We will be very quiet,' he added.

'He scared the living daylights out of me,' Lucy admitted as she began to sort out the straw to lie on.

'He's a gentle giant, really,' Troy said.

They stacked the straw into two comfortable bundles side by side.

Lucy yawned loudly. 'I can't wait to get into bed.'

'There's no better place when you are tired,' Troy said.

They snuggled down into their little straw beds.

'I hope Chico is all right,' Lucy murmured drowsily.

'I'm sure he will be fine. Night, Lucy,' Troy whispered. But there was no reply. She was fast asleep.

Somewhere outside, in the darkness, an owl hooted.

They woke early.

'Have we anything left to eat?' Troy said, hopefully.

Lucy looked in her haversack and brought out a small packet of chocolate biscuits and two small cartons of fruit juice. 'This is all we have left,' she said quietly.

'Morning, I hope you slept well,' Billy Bull said. 'I am awake. You do not have to whisper.'

'Morning,' they both chorused.

'I wonder if you would mind doing me a favour?' Billy bull said, pacing the floor.

'Anything, pal,' Troy said. 'What would you like me to do?'

'I have the most irritating itch on my back and wondered if you would mind giving it a scratch?'

'Not at all,' Troy said. 'But I can't reach right up there from down here.' He looked around and found a small stool to stand on and a garden rake with big teeth. 'This should do the trick.' As soon as he was ready, he began to rub the rake vigorously along Billy's back, just like a comb.

'That is wonderful,' Billy roared, wriggling in delight.

Lucy couldn't help laughing. 'That's the funniest thing I have ever seen.'

'You can stop now,' Billy Bull said. 'My itch has quite gone.'

Troy grinned widely at him. 'Any time,' he said, laughing. He looked around. 'We'll leave everything exactly as we found it, so no one will ever know we have been here.'

Troy put the rake and the stool back where he had found them. He picked up a handful of straw and began to scatter it about. Lucy picked up a handful of straw and playfully threw it at Troy.

'You will be sorry you did that,' he yelled, laughing, and threw a handful back at her. 'Stop it! Stop it,' he said as handfuls of straw landed on his head. 'Enough! Enough!' Troy chuckled. 'You win.'

'That was fun,' Lucy said, brushing the straw from her hair and clothes.

'Can't see any fun in that,' Billy Bull snorted.

This made them laugh even more.

They left the barn in the same state they had found it in and said goodbye to their friend Billy Bull.

Popping their heads out for a quick look to ensure no one was around, they spotted the farmer in the distance with his back to them, herding his sheep.

'Come on,' Troy said. 'Let us make a run for it.'

They had just left the safety of the barn when the farmer suddenly looked up and saw them running off.

'Hey! You, there! Stop! I want a word with you,' he shouted. 'I don't want the likes of you stealing my good eggs and chickens without paying for them.'

Chico came bounding out of the woods to meet them.

'Run! Chico, Run!' they cried.

The little monkey did as he was told.

They did not stop running until they had left the farmer far behind them.

THE TEDDY BEAR'S PICNIC

Lucy and Troy stopped to rest beside a stream that belonged to the deep river that ran away into the distance. They had shaken off the meanies that had been following them.

'Oh, this is nice,' Lucy said, looking around.

'We can stay here and get some rest.' Troy said.

'Who do you think was following us?'

'I have no doubt it was the meanies after the reward money. I have a price on my head, remember.'

'Well, they won't catch us now,' she said.

'I didn't know you could run like that. You were as fast as a racehorse.'

'I always came first in the school races,' she exclaimed proudly. 'And I have lots of medals at home to prove it.'

'Have you really?'

'Yes. I have.' Lucy smiled.

'You are clever.'

It was a lovely day. The sun was shining, the birds were twittering in the trees, and flowers bloomed everywhere.

'Fancy a little paddle?' Troy said with a grin and began to take off his sensible shoes and brown socks.

'Yes, I do,' Lucy said, taking off her sandals and pink socks.

They both stepped into the shallow water. Chico sat on the bank quietly watching.

'Oh, this is nice,' Lucy said, wriggling her toes in the water.

'It's smashing, isn't it?'

They splashed about for a while, then sat in the shade of the trees and let their feet dry naturally in the sunshine before putting their shoes and socks back on. They were surprised to see a big brown mama bear and her cubs heading towards them.

'Shush,' Troy said softly in her ear. 'We don't want to upset mama bear.'

Lucy sat quietly beside him, not daring to make a sound, knowing they were in great danger of being killed at any second.

The mama bear sat down on the soft green grass a few feet away. The baby bears began to knock each other about playfully and climbed trees. Mama bear sat contentedly watching them fool around.

Suddenly a baby bear fell out of the tree he had been climbing and slipped into the river. Lucy gasped when she saw what had happened.

Troy jumped up and raced to the rescue. He took a flying leap into the river and grabbed the baby bear before it was swept away by the fast-moving current.

Lucy watched in alarm as he began to swim bravely back to the bank with the baby bear safely clinging onto his back. As soon as he drew near, a huge paw grabbed them both and hauled them out of the water.

'You have risked your life to save my little Dinky,' mama bear cried, hugging the cold, wet, frightened little bear in her arms.

Lucy helped a gasping Troy to his feet. 'You are so brave,' she said shakily. 'I thought you were going to both drown.' She had forgotten to be afraid of mama bear in all the excitement.

'Thank you for saving his life,' mama bear said.

'Would you care to join us at the teddy bear's picnic?'

Lucy clapped her hands together. 'Oh, yes, please.'

'That would be marvellous,' Troy said, placing his clothes to dry in the hot sun.

'I am known as mama bear,' she said as the baby bears came close to her. 'These are my children. That is Beano, and he is the eldest. Ruffles is next in line, and these two are my twins, Boxy and Stalk, and my little one here is Dinky, who you saved from a watery grave and is always getting into trouble.' She put little Dinky down.

'I'm Troy, and this is my friend Lucy.'

'Hello,' Lucy said as a little hand crept into hers, and she saw it was one of the bear cubs. He was so sweet, and she wanted to put her arms around him and hug him but was unsure if mama bear would object, so she smiled gently at him instead.

They sat together and waited as mama bear put a paw into her straw basket and brought out a red and white checked tablecloth. She spread it out on the grass in front of them, then reaching into her basket again, took out the honey pots and pulled off the lids before handing each little bear a jar of honey. Then she gave Troy and Lucy one each.

'Thank you,' they both said quietly.

They all began to eat.

'Ooh, this is delicious,' Lucy said, dipping her finger into the honey pot.

Troy was far too busy eating to say anything at all.

There was the sound of slurping and licking as all the little bears enjoyed their honey. But the honey pots were soon empty.

'Thank you, Mama,' the little bears shouted as

soon as they had finished eating and ran off to play.

'What lovely manners they have,' Lucy said, watching them scamper away.

'We've had a marvellous time,' Troy said and licked the last of the honey from the spoon.

Lucy grinned. 'I will treasure this moment all my life.'

Mama bear tidied up. 'Before you go, I have something to tell you,' she said, looking around and sniffing the air. 'You are not alone in these woods, and I sense danger. Someone means you harm. You must leave now. I will wait here to greet them.'

'It must be the meanies,' Troy cried in alarm.

'Oh, no! I thought we had lost them,' Lucy said.

Troy jumped to his feet. 'We must get away from here.'

They quickly ran off into the woods but had not got far when they heard a mighty roar.

Troy chuckled. 'That's mama bear greeting our enemies. The meanies will get the biggest fright of their life when they see her, but she won't harm them,' he added.

Lucy grimaced. 'Serves them right.'

They carried on walking at a brisk pace.

'I can't believe we've been to a teddy bear's picnic,' Lucy said sometime later. 'I shall never forget it as long as I live.'

'It was marvellous,' Troy agreed.

Chico had been hiding in the trees, a safe distance from the bears, but he came running over to them once they were alone.

The little monkey began to chatter away, making Troy chuckle with glee.

Lucy smiled. 'What's so funny?'

'Chico said if we hadn't saved her little bear, then mama bear would have gobbled us up too.'

They laughed until their sides ached.

THE MAN WITH HIS POTS AND PANS

Much later, they turned a bend in the road and saw a man up ahead driving a pony and trap. They could hear his pots and pans clanging as he trotted along.

'I would love a ride in that,' Lucy said. Chico, tucked cosily inside her jacket, gave a contented sigh.

Troy stopped. 'So would I.'

'Come on, let's ask him,' she said.

They ran up to him.

The man saw them coming. 'You are strangers around these parts.' He frowned. 'What is it you want?'

'We would love to ride in your cart,' Lucy said, smiling sweetly at him.

The man smiled back. 'Hop aboard. A bit of company would be most welcome.'

Troy and Lucy jumped up beside him.

'I'm known around these parts as Trotter,' he said.

'I'm called Lucy, and this is my friend Troy.'

'My pleasure,' Trotter said.

Chico popped his head out to look around.

Trotter's eyes widened. 'Here, just a minute, is that a monkey you got there?'

'This is Chico,' Lucy said, holding him close. 'He won't hurt you,' she added with a cheeky grin.

The time passed pleasantly until they came to a crossroads and turned off into a nearby field.

'I must rest here a while,' Trotter said, climbing from his cart. Troy and Lucy jumped down together.

Trotter stroked his horse gently on the forehead. 'We've come a long way, haven't we, old girl?' he spoke lovingly to the animal before turning to face Troy and Lucy. 'Will you be going or staying?'

'We must leave you here,' Troy said.

'Thank you for the ride,' Lucy said. 'It was nice meeting you.'

Trotter watched them leave. 'Goodbye and good luck,' he called after them.

'Goodbye,' they both shouted as they started their journey again.

THE PIRATES

Lucy and Troy came to a harbour leading out to sea full of small boats and sailing ships.

'How will you know which is our ship?' Lucy said.

'I will know when I see it,' Troy replied with great confidence.

A big sailing ship with the name, *Gauntlet* on the side was coming into the harbour.

'That's it! That's the one!' he cried excitedly. 'Come on.'

The Gauntlet had docked nearby, and there was no one around. The mist swirled in, giving them the perfect cover to hurry down to the harbour and duck down behind packing cases.

'Let us make a run for it,' Troy whispered.

Lucy slipped Chico inside her jacket. 'Not a sound now, Chico,' she whispered, and the little monkey seemed to understand and lay still and silent in the warmth of her coat.

They ran up the gangplank and hid beneath a large tarpaulin. They did not have long to wait before they heard the ship's engines. The ship began to roll about in the windy weather, making them seasick.

'Land ahoy,' a voice cried.

Lucy and Troy popped their heads out to look around. A flag with skull and crossbones was flying from the mast.

They quickly ducked back under cover, but it was too late. They had been seen.

Troy gasped. 'Oh, no. We've come aboard a pirate ship.'

Lucy's eyes widened. With Chico still inside her

jacket, she whispered, 'What do we do now?'

They heard a gruff voice call out, 'WE HAVE STOWAWAYS ABOARD!'

'We've been seen!' Troy said, looking horrified.

'GRAB 'EM LADS!' the pirate captain bellowed.

They were pulled out into the open and surrounded by the rough-looking crew.

'What we gonna do with 'em, lads?' the pirate captain shouted.

'Make 'em walk the plank,' one eye said.

A guffaw of laughter went up.

'All in agreement, say aye,' the pirate captain roared.

The pirates yelled boisterously.

'AYE, CAPTAIN!'

'You can't do that,' Troy snarled.

'Take your filthy hands off me,' Lucy yelled.

They both struggled as they were grabbed from behind.

They were shown no mercy as the pirates laughingly pushed them onto the narrow plank of wood that dangled over an angry sea. They were prodded along to the very end of the plank by a long pole and were in danger of falling off.

'We are all going to die here,' Lucy said, sobbing and struggling to keep her balance.

Troy looked desperately around and saw a massive cormorant in the sky.

'Help!' he called, using his magic powers. 'Please save us!'

The cormorant flew straight towards them and landed high up on the ship's mast. He looked directly at Troy with his beady little eyes before flapping his great wings and flying down to land next to them.

The pirates stared in horror at the giant bird.

'It's a cormorant!' one eye said.

'That's bad luck,' another pirate said.

'We are doomed,' another cried.

They were all terrified.

'Quick,' Troy shouted to Lucy. 'Jump on.'

She quickly climbed up onto the cormorant. Its back was as broad as a horse.

Troy leapt on behind her. 'Hang on tight!' he cried.

The cormorant flapped his great wings and flew into the air. Then, higher and higher, they soared into the sky and over the vast expanse of water. The pirates stared up in amazement as they flew away.

Troy and Lucy breathed a sigh of relief as soon as they landed safely on the ground.

Lucy smiled. 'Oh, I enjoyed that.'

'Marvellous,' Troy said, chuckling. He turned to the cormorant. 'We can't thank you enough for saving our lives.'

'Anytime, matey,' the cormorant said. 'Now, if there is nothing else you need. I'll be off, and a good day to you.'

'Goodbye. Goodbye,' Lucy and Troy chorused.

They watched him fly away and out of sight.

'Isn't he wonderful,' she whispered.

'The best,' agreed Troy.

Chico popped his head out and began to chatter away.

'Chico said he doesn't like pirates but likes their gold earrings. Look, he has one in his hand,' an astonished Troy said as they howled with laughter.

THE LITTLE COTTAGE IN THE WOODS

Lucy and Troy entered a deep dark wood. They had gone some distance when they saw a cottage.

Troy pointed at it. 'Look!' he said.

'Oh, what a sweet little cottage,' Lucy said.

Troy smiled. 'We'll sleep there tonight.'

They headed towards it. Chico jumped to the ground and ran off.

'Chico,' Lucy cried. 'Where's he gone?'

'He likes to sleep in the trees,' Troy said. 'He is a little monkey, after all.' They both smiled.

Lucy tapped lightly on the cottage door, and it slowly swung open.

'Enter,' called a voice from inside.

They went straight in.

A white-haired old lady sat by the fireside. She looked up as they entered and smiled sweetly at them. 'Hello,' she said pleasantly. 'What can I do for you?'

'Can we stay here tonight?' Lucy asked, hopefully.

The old lady smiled. 'Strangers are always welcome.'

'Thank you,' Troy said, and a very odd feeling came over him that he couldn't explain.

'I expect you would both like a bite to eat?'

'Yes, please,' Lucy said.

The delicious smell of cooking from the pot on the open fire made both their mouths water.

The old lady filled two bowls with soup. 'You must have some of my homemade mushroom soup. Sit at the table, and I'll bring it over.'

Troy and Lucy sat at a small table by the window.

The sweet old lady placed a bowl of soup in front of each of them.

'Thank you,' they both said, smiling.

'It looks delicious,' Lucy said.

'This is a treat,' Troy said.

They began to eat.

'I will lock the door. We don't want any burglars creeping in when we are asleep in our beds,' the sweet old lady said, turning the key in the lock. She began to sing in a funny little sing-song voice, and strange music filled the cottage.

Troy and Lucy had finished their soup and fallen asleep.

'Oh, the master will love you,' cackled the witch who had pretended to be a sweet old lady. 'There be plenty of meat on your bones to enjoy.'

She picked up the broomstick she had kept hidden and flew away into the darkness. She was soon gone.

THE WITCH'S SPELL

They woke up locked in a cage.

'What's happened to us?' Lucy said as she rattled the cage noisily.

'We have been taken for fools,' Troy said angrily. 'The witch lives here.'

'Are you telling me that sweet old lady is a witch?'

The sound of distant drums came from the forest. It was an evil sound that was terrifying to hear.

A big ginger cat jumped down from the windowsill where she had been watching them. 'I knew she would catch you in the end,' the cat said. 'She always does, you know.'

'And how would you know that?' Troy said.

'The witch put a magic spell on my Mistress and turned her into a statue. That's her on the windowsill, and I must stay with her. I'm called Ginger, but the witch calls me scraggy bones,' the cat added.

'Can you get us out of here?' Troy said, hopefully.

'No, I'm afraid not,' Ginger said sadly. 'The witch hides the key to the lock in a drawer, and I can't open it.'

At that moment, a little face appeared at the slightly open window.

They both looked up.

'It's Chico,' Lucy said. 'Come on, Chico! Help us!'

Troy grinned. 'He will save us.'

Chico wriggled his way inside.

'Get the key, Chico. It's in the drawer,' Troy said, pointing to it.

Chico ran to do his bidding and returned with the key in his little hand. Troy took it from him, quickly opened the door, and set them free.

'Oh, you clever little monkey,' Lucy said as Chico jumped into her loving arms, and she held him close to her heart.

'Well done, Chico,' Troy said. 'You are a brave little monkey.'

'Let's get out of here.' Lucy made for the door.

'There's something I must do first,' Troy said and hurried over to the windowsill.

He picked up the statue with the glassy-eyed stare and placed it gently on the ground. Troy waved his hands about and said the magic words, then puff! The statue was no more, and a lovely young girl with long golden hair stood in her place. Green eyes stared back at them, full of gratitude.

'Oh, I am me again,' the girl said joyfully and quickly scooped Ginger into her arms. 'He wouldn't leave me, you know, even though he was slowly starving to death. I can't thank you enough for saving both of our lives. Please tell me who you are?'

'I'm Troy, and this is Lucy with her pet monkey, Chico.'

'I'm Dolly, and this is my cat, Ginger.'

The sound of distant drums had stopped.

'Let's get out of here,' Troy said. 'Before the witch comes back.'

They ran for their lives and didn't stop until they were far away. Then, finally, they stopped at the edge of the forest. In the distance, they could see a church steeple and rows of small cottages dotted about.

'That is where I live,' Dolly said. 'Where are you headed for?' she enquired politely.

'We are going to my home, and we will soon be there.' Troy smiled widely at her.

'And where is your home, Lucy?'

'I live in the orphanage until my parents are found,' she said. 'They were lost at sea, and everyone is out looking for them. I know they are still alive somewhere, and when they find them, I am going back home.'

'Oh, dear,' Dolly said. 'I hope they find your parents soon.'

'I'm sure they will,' Troy said firmly. 'But until they are found, Lucy is coming home with me.'

Lucy smiled. 'I'm looking forward to seeing where Troy lives.'

'It's time I went home. My parents must be missing me,' Dolly said, eager to be off. 'I will never forget you. Goodbye.'

'Goodbye,' they said.

They watched Dolly run down the hill towards home with Ginger held lovingly in her arms.

'They are both safe now,' Troy said, smiling.

'It's time we were off too.'

They set off on their journey once more.

THE LITTLE TREE HOUSE

Lucy and Troy were deep in the countryside when they heard someone shouting.

'OUCH! THAT HURTS! GET OFF ME!

'Someone's in trouble, and we must help him,' Troy said.

Lucy and Troy took off at a run.

They could see two bullies beating a poor helpless little leprechaun half their size.

'LET HIM GO!' Troy shouted, waving a big stick at them that he had picked up along the way.

'GET OFF HIM, YOU BULLIES!' Lucy cried as they raced towards them.

Chico was running along beside them, screeching madly. The two bullies saw them coming and ran for their lives. The poor leprechaun fell to the ground in a dead faint. They rushed over to him, and Troy crouched low to feel his pulse.

'Have they killed him?' Lucy asked.

'No, he is still alive.'

The leprechaun soon came around but gasped and edged away from the pair.

'We are not going to hurt you,' Troy said and helped him to his feet.

'You are safe now,' Lucy said.

He grinned. 'Thank you for saving my life,' the leprechaun said. 'You certainly scared off the bullies. I nearly died of fright myself when I saw you coming.' He chortled with glee. 'I've never seen anything like it.'

They were soon all laughing merrily.

'I must know who you are,' the Leprechaun

'I'm called Troy.'

'And I'm Lucy, and this is Chico.'

'My friends call me Toby. I live nearby. Will you join me for a bite to eat? You must be hungry after all that ranting and raving.' He chuckled loudly.

It set them off laughing again.

'I'd like that,' Lucy said.

'I have worked up quite an appetite,' Troy said, grinning.

They walked companionably along until they reached a thick part of the forest.

'That's where I live,' Toby said, pointing to the treetops. They looked up and could see a little door hidden in the trees. He untied a rope ladder covered in greenery. 'Up we go,' he said and swiftly climbed the rope ladder.

Lucy and Troy followed him, with Chico swinging up behind them.

Toby threw open his arms and smiled. 'Welcome to my home. Please find a seat.'

A jackdaw flew in through the open window. 'Caw, Caw,' he called, flapping his wings before perching on Toby's shoulder.

'This is Jackie,' Toby said. 'He keeps me company and warns me of strangers approaching.'

Jackie gave a loud caw, caw, and flew over onto Troy's shoulder and began nibbling his ear.

'Oh, don't do that!' he said, laughing. 'You are tickling me.'

It made them all giggle.

'I see he has found a friend,' Toby said. 'I best get us something to eat.' He disappeared into the little open kitchen and soon returned carrying a tray laden with fruits from the forest. He placed a jug of juice on the table for Lucy and Troy. 'Tuck in,' Toby said.

'These strawberries are delicious,' Troy said, smacking his lips.

'Have another one.'

'Don't mind if I do.'

'So is this plum,' Lucy said and took another bite.

Chico nibbled on a banana but kept a wary eye on the Jackdaw.

'You must taste my homemade blackberry juice,' Toby said and poured each of them a glass. 'Would you mind telling me where you're bound for?'

'I'm going home,' Troy said, 'and Lucy is coming with me. I have missed my home so much and can't wait to see all my friends again.'

'Well, why did you leave if you like it so much?'

'The meanies captured me and sold me to the circus.' Troy told him all about it. 'I escaped, and Lucy found me hiding in the garden and hid me in the cellar of her home,' he added. 'She saved my life.'

Toby looked at Lucy and smiled. It was as if he could see into her heart and knew everything about her. 'We find friends in the strangest of places,' he said. 'And we all need a friend in times of trouble.'

Lucy smiled back at him.

'And what about you, Lucy? Where do you live?'

'I have to stay in an orphanage until my parents are found,' she said and sniffed. 'Everyone thinks they drowned at sea, but I know they are safe, and when they find them, I'm going home.'

Toby furrowed his brow. 'What a terrible thing to happen, but I'm sure you're right. They will be found safe and well,' he added quickly.

'I'm sure of it,' Troy said, gently patting Lucy's arm. 'We just have to wait a little longer until they are found.'

'Would you like to try one of my coconut cakes,' Toby said and passed them one each. 'I am considering selling them on the market and would like to know what you think.'

They took a small coconut cake and bit into it.

'They taste delicious,' Lucy said, feeling quite light-hearted.

Troy gave a knowing smile. 'These are magic,' he cried and howled with laughter.

Toby began to chuckle. They were soon all laughing heartily.

It was time to say goodbye.

Troy and Lucy climbed back down the rope ladder one at a time. Chico swung from the tree branches until he reached the ground.

They stood at the bottom and waved up at Toby in the tree tops, and he waved back. He pulled up his rope ladder, and then he was gone.

The little tree house was hidden from sight.

THE FAIRGROUND

They left the tree house far behind them, with Chico swinging from tree to tree in the lush green forest.

'I can hear music,' Troy said, stopping to listen. 'It sounds like a fairground.'

'Come on, let's see where it's coming from,' Lucy said eagerly.

They followed the music and saw a big colourful fairground in the middle of a field.

'Oh, look at all the rides!' Lucy said. 'We must have a ride on something!'

Chico had disappeared.

'He keeps wandering off, doesn't he?' Lucy said, looking around.

'He loves swinging in the trees,' Troy said. 'He will come back when he is ready.'

The fairground was a busy place with happy families enjoying themselves. The sound of children's laughter filled the air.

All the rides had long queues except for the ghost train. Only a few brave stragglers were waiting to go in.

'Let's ride on the ghost train,' Lucy cried. 'I dare you.'

Troy gave a wicked grin. 'Come on, then.'

'I have just enough pocket money left for a ticket,' she added, taking some money out of her little red purse.

They joined a queue and climbed into the empty car when their turn came.

'Hold on tight,' the operator called as they set off into the gloom.

Ghostly sounds and strange apparitions loomed out of the darkness. Troy shrieked with laughter, and Lucy screamed with pretended fright as they made their way slowly through the pitch-black tunnel. Skeletons with red eyes hung on either side of them, and cobwebs brushed their faces as they passed.

They didn't know two men were waiting for them in the darkness. Then, suddenly, a rope was thrown around them, and they were pulled out of the car and dragged to one side as the little car sped off.

'Gotcha!' a gruff voice said.

'Ouch! That hurt,' Troy shouted.

'Get off me,' Lucy said.

They were swiftly tied up.

'We've been kidnapped!' Troy cried.

'Help! Help!' Lucy shouted at the top of her voice. A cruel hand was forced over her mouth to shut her up.

'You'll keep your gob shut if you know what's good for you,' an angry voice bellowed.

'Get a move on, Bud and let's get them out of here,' his accomplice said.

'Okay, okay, keep your hair on, Jakey boy,' he snarled back.

Troy and Lucy were bundled outside into a quiet back street. It was daylight, but there was no one about. They stared at the two angry men with a look of horror.

'Come on, move it,' Bud said.

A dirty rag had been put over their mouths to silence them. They were taken to a horse-drawn caravan nearby and thrown in the back like two sacks of coal. Bud jumped in behind them and tied them both to a rail.

'You won't escape this time,' he said, pulling the curtain across so no one could see inside. Then he jumped back out to ride up front with Jakey boy.

It all happened so quickly.

CAUGHT IN A TRAP

'Giddy up!' Jakey boy shouted.

The horse set off at a fast pace. Troy and Lucy bounced along like tennis balls, and then it was over. The journey had come to an end.

Bud and Jakey boy climbed into the back of the caravan. Troy and Lucy were quickly pulled out and their gags removed.

Bud grinned. 'Shout all you want. No one will hear you in this place.'

Lucy shivered when she saw his toothless smile.

Troy and Lucy looked around at the horrible place they were in. Rocks and boulders and deep holes were everywhere. There was not a blade of grass, and no birds sang. It was a silent place.

They were taken to the entrance of a cave.

'Oh no,' Troy said when he realised where they were taking them. 'Oh, please, let Lucy go, and I will do whatever you want!'

'I'm not going in there!' Lucy protested. She hated dark places.

Bud growled. 'Oh, yes you are. We can't let you go and spill the beans.'

Troy struggled to free himself. 'There is no need for this.'

'Struggle all you want,' Bud said. 'Dead or alive makes no difference to us. It's back to the circus for you.'

Jakey boy rubbed his hands together gleefully. 'We are going to claim the reward for your capture. The ringmaster will pay well to get you back.'

They were pushed into the cave and tied up.

Troy struggled violently to free himself when the gold medallion suddenly came loose from his clothing.

'What's that around his neck?' Bud said.

Jakey boy gasped. 'I've seen that before.'

Bud grabbed hold of Troy. 'Where did you get that medallion?' he demanded.

'An old woman gave it to me,' Troy said. 'She said it belonged to her very wise husband.'

Bud grabbed it as it swung loosely around Troy's neck, but the chain refused to break and became so hot it burnt his hand. 'Ouch,' Bud cried and quickly let it go.

Chico came running towards them, screeching wildly, leaping onto Lucy's shoulders, and wrapping its little arms protectively around her neck.

The two men drew back in fear.

'That's Chico!' Jakey boy yelled. 'What's he doing here?'

'He must have been hiding on the caravan's roof,' Bud said.

'That little monkey belonged to the old woman's husband too,' Jakey boy said, looking terrified. 'We must let them go, or we will be cursed for life!'

'There's only one thing to do,' Bud said. He pulled out a knife and swished the air with it.

Troy and Lucy stared at him, too frightened to move, as Bud grabbed the ropes and cut them free.

'Get out of here.'

They ran for their lives.

*****

'The medallion saved us,' Lucy said once they were

safely away.

Troy smiled. 'Chico saved us too.'

'Where is he now?' Lucy added, looking around.

'Oh, he won't be far away,' Troy said. 'He is a true friend to us and the old woman, too,' he added softly. 'They have both saved our lives.'

He touched the medallion and safely tucked it back inside his clothes.

THE DESERTED VILLAGE

They soon came upon a village.

Troy threw his arms wide. 'This is my home in Havenlea.'

'Oh, it's heavenly!' Lucy stared in amazement at the beautiful surroundings. 'Look, there is a little fairy,' she said.

A sweet little face was looking down at them from the leafy branches of a tree.

'Hello,' Troy said pleasantly. 'I'm back.'

'Danger lies ahead,' the little fairy said in a sing-song voice, and then she was gone.

'What?' Troy said, but there was only silence. He frowned. 'Fairies can cause more trouble than an itch. Come on, Lucy.'

They hurried along.

The village sat nestled in the hills. It was a pretty sight with rows of gaily painted cottages in neat little rows. The trees were laden with fruit, and strawberries grew as big as footballs. Mushrooms the size of dinner plates sprouted all around, flowers of all colours were in full bloom, and the bird song was everywhere.

'Wow!' Lucy gasped, gazing about her in wonder. 'This is amazing.'

'It's such a happy place,' Troy said. 'Come on. You must meet my friends.'

They hurried along the country lanes and entered the village smiling and laughing.

Troy stopped. 'Where has everyone gone?'

The place was deserted. Lucy waited as Troy knocked on the doors of the cottages, but there was no one home.

'What's happened here?' he cried. 'Where have they all gone?'

'Look,' Lucy said, pointing to a smoking chimney.

A plume of smoke drifted lazily upwards from a little cottage in the woods.

'Someone is in there!' Troy said.

They crept towards it.

Troy pushed open the door. 'Who is in here?'

'Go away,' cried a voice trembling with fear.

'Sammy,' Troy said. 'Is that you?'

'Who are you, and how do you know my name?'

'I'm Troy, don't you remember me?'

'Is that my friend, Troy?' the voice said, and a little elf came out of hiding. 'I can see it really is you,' he said. 'But who is that with you?'

'This is Lucy and Chico, her little monkey. Lucy, this is my friend, Sammy.'

They were quickly introduced.

'Now tell me what has been going on?' Troy said. 'And where is everyone?'

'Oh, dear. Oh, dear,' Sammy wailed. 'I will never forget it for as long as I live.'

'Start at the beginning and tell me everything.'

'Well,' Sammy said, pulling himself together, 'the Trolls pounced on the village and took everyone prisoner. Oh, it was horrible!'

Troy gasped. 'What! Why did they do that?'

'They have taken them to work in the gold mines,' Sammy said.

'How do you know all this?' Troy asked.

'I was in the hen coop collecting eggs when they attacked, and I heard them talking. So I hid there until they had gone.' The tears ran down his face like waterfalls. 'I couldn't save them,' he sobbed.

'I quite understand,' Troy said.

Lucy looked at them both. 'What is he talking about?'

'Trolls are spiteful, greedy creatures and love anything shiny, especially gold,' Sammy said. 'They have a gold mine but are too lazy to work it themselves.'

Troy made a fist. 'They are not going to get away with it. How long have they been gone?'

'They were taken seven moons ago. They are lost to us now,' Sammy wailed. 'All gone forever.'

Troy stamped his foot. 'Oh, shut up and let me think. We must make a plan if we are to save them.'

'Oh, do you think we can?' Sammy said.

Troy clicked his fingers. 'I have an idea. Do you still have your air balloon?'

'Of course I do. Why do you ask?'

'Where is it?'

'In green acres meadow where it always is.' Sammy said.

'I must see it.'

'I will show you where it is.'

'Where are we going?' Lucy asked as they hurried away.

'You'll see!' Troy said as they all ran together.

THE FLYING BALLOON

They all stared at a huge orange air balloon floating a few feet off the ground. The basket it was tied to was held down by thick ropes staked into the ground. 'We are going to find out where the mine is,' Troy said. 'Then we are going to save everyone.'

Sammy clapped his hands together. 'We can go now.'

'I would love to go up in that,' Lucy said excitedly.

Sammy looked at her. 'Is she coming too?' he asked.

Troy grinned. 'Try and stop her.'

'Quick, jump in,' Sammy shouted, untying the ropes fastened to the ground.

They all climbed in and began to float high into the air. Chico was strangely silent, wrapped in Lucy's arms.

The wind blew them gently along, high into the sky over rivers, trees and mountains.

Troy looked into the distance. 'Do you know the way, Sammy?'

'I do,' he said. 'The wind is blowing in the right direction.' He looked at his compass. 'I came this way once before and saw the gold mine and the trolls. It gave me an awful fright.'

They drifted leisurely along for a while.

'We have arrived,' Sammy said quietly.

They all looked down at the ground far below and

saw the entrance to the mine. The trolls were everywhere.

They stared wide-eyed as a long line of elves, gnomes and pixies came stumbling out of the mine. They were almost bent double with the weight of heavy bags strapped to their backs. They looked exhausted as they made their way to the railway track and empty wagons. They unloaded the heavy loads of gold into them before stumbling weakly back into the mine, closely watched by the trolls.

'Oh, the poor things,' Lucy whispered.

Sammy shook his head. 'I have never seen anything so cruel in all my life.'

'The gold is all they care about,' Troy muttered. 'They need to be taught a lesson they will never forget.'

Sammy's heart was breaking, and tears weren't far away.

They kept their voices low.

'What they need is a rocket up the bum!' Lucy said.

Troy was astounded. 'What a brilliant idea.'

'Oh, why didn't I think of that?' Sammy said.

They chuckled and laughed gleefully together.

Lucy frowned. 'What's the matter with you both?'

Troy rubbed his hands together. 'Thanks to you, we know how to save our friends. We must ask Dynamo for help. Any idea where we can find him, Sammy?'

'I know where his home is, and I will take us there.' Sammy started messing about with the balloon workings. As the balloon filled with air, they rose high up into the sky.

They floated higher and higher until they were soon out of sight.

SAVED BY A GIANT

Troy looked up and sighed. 'There's a storm brewing,' he said.

The sky was dark and threatening. Chico was silent as he stared about him with his button-brown eyes. The rain poured down, and thunder and lightning streaked across the sky. Soon they were soaked to the skin as the wild wind whirled them madly about in the little basket. They hung on grimly, terrified of falling out. A vast mountain loomed before them, and they were certain to crash. Then an enormous hand reached out and held the basket steady to stop them from falling out.

'I will help you,' the friendly giant said.

They soon realised he meant no harm as the basket became still while the storm raged around them. The giant held the basket gently in the palm of his hand until the storm was over.

'You best be on your way now,' the kindly giant said.

'Thank you for saving our lives,' Troy said gratefully.

The giant smiled. 'You are welcome. You little people should take more care of yourselves.' He blew them gently on their way.

'Goodbye,' they all cried as they journeyed high into the sky.

DYNAMO TO THE RESCUE

They landed with a slight bump, and Troy and Lucy quickly jumped out to help Sammy tie the basket securely to the ground.

'Come on,' Troy said. 'We haven't much time.'

They took off at a sprint. Lucy held a silent Chico in her arms as they raced along. Soon they approached the house set low in the hills.

Sammy knocked loudly on the door, but there was no reply. 'Oh, no. There is no one in. All is lost,' he wailed.

Troy pointed his finger. 'What is that grey building over there?'

'That's Dynamo's workshop,' Sammy said. 'It's where he makes all his fireworks.'

'Come on, then, what are we waiting for?' Troy said. We must take as many fireworks as we can carry.'

Lucy and Sammy hurried after him.

'You can't steal his fireworks,' Sammy shouted.

'It's the only way to save our friends,' Troy said.

They read the sign on the door.

BUSY BODIES KEEP OUT.

Troy pushed the door open, and they all went inside.

'Can't you read?' a voice bellowed from inside.

'Oh, there you are,' Sammy said, pleased to see his old friend Dynamo.

Troy stepped forward. 'We need your help to save our friends.'

'You are the only one who can help us now,' Sammy said.

They told him everything as Lucy stood close by with Chico on her shoulder, as quiet as a little mouse.

'They are not going to get away with it,' Dynamo growled. 'We'll teach them a lesson they will never forget.' He pointed to rows of boxes. 'These are the best fireworks I have ever made. We'll take everything and put in the back of my jeep what we can't carry.'

They all walked out in single file carrying a full box each. The jeep was soon full of boxes of fireworks.

'That's the lot,' Dynamo said. 'Off you go, and I will catch up.'

They all set off running. Lucy carried Chico close to her heart as they raced back to the balloon. Dynamo followed them in his jeep. The fireworks were quickly placed in the basket, and they all jumped in.

Sammy untied the ropes to set the balloon free. 'Up and away,' he cried as they floated gently away.

They were soon high up in the clear blue sky.

Dynamo grinned. 'Oh, this is wonderful,' he said. 'I didn't know it could be such fun!'

And they all smiled at him.

THE TROLLS

The balloon landed on the ground, and they all scrambled out. Sammy secured the balloon to the ground where it would not be seen.

'We are in Troll land now,' Troy whispered a warning. 'It's this way.'

They marched along in single file with arms full of fireworks. Dynamo was last in line with rockets tucked neatly under his arms and a massive grin on his face, ready for battle.

It was getting dark, but the moon shone down on them, helping them to see where they were going. They crept as close to the mine as they dared, hid in the bushes and peeped out.

'Look, there's a Troll,' Troy whispered and pointed to a Troll standing guard at the entrance to the mine.

'We'll have to find a way to get him out of the way,' Dynamo said.

'How are we going to do that?' Lucy said.

'That's how we get them away,' Troy whispered, pointing to the train standing at the station nearby.

A whistle sounded, and all the elves, gnomes and pixies were led out of the mine. They were taken to a hut and quickly locked inside by the trolls. The key was taken away and put on a shelf out of sight before the trolls wandered off, grunting and snorting together.

'That must be the sleeping quarters,' Troy said quietly. 'All we have to do now is grab the key, open the door, and get them out of there.'

Dynamo frowned. 'They won't know it's us coming to rescue them,' he said.

'We have to find a way to let them know it's us,' Sammy said, 'or all will be lost if the trolls find out.'

'How are we going to do that?' Just as Troy asked the question, a fox appeared.

'Excuse me,' the fox said, 'but what are you all doing here hiding like rabbits?'

'We are here to rescue our friends from certain death,' Troy said in a low voice. 'They are prisoners of the trolls and made to work in the mine.'

'Nasty creatures, those trolls, always causing trouble. Why only yesterday they caught my friend Beasley and locked him in a cage,' the fox said, swishing his tail. 'Look, he's over there.'

They peeped out and could see a little fox locked in a cage.

'They are going to eat him for their dinner, and there is nothing I can do to save him, and he has little ones at home,' he added sadly.

'We will not allow that to happen,' Troy whispered. 'We will find a way to set him free.'

'Oh, I hope you can, we grew up together, and he is my best friend,' the fox said. 'Can I return the favour in any way?'

They huddled closer together, and Troy spoke quietly, 'We would be grateful if you could warn our friends that we are here to rescue them. They are locked in that hut.' He pointed to it. 'You're good at creeping about,' Troy added, smiling in the darkness.

'I am happy to help. I'm not called Foxy for nothing.' He dashed off.

Troy turned to Chico and said softly, 'We need your help too.'

Chico looked at him with his eyes wide.

'I know what a clever little monkey you are. Do you

think you can unlock the cage and set the Fox free?'

Chico ran swiftly and silently away.

In no time, he was back with a fox by his side.

'I didn't know I had so many friends,' the little fox said. 'Would you mind telling me your names so I may thank you properly?'

They whispered their names to him.

Foxy appeared out of the darkness. 'I have passed your message on.'

'We are grateful to you,' Troy said. 'But how did you manage it?'

'I crawled through a little hole in the ground,' Foxy said. 'I don't think they will last much longer in the state they were in.' He swished his tail angrily before turning to Beasley. 'You are out then. I'm glad about that.'

'What is going on here?' Beasley said.

They whispered together in the darkness.

'Fireworks are dangerous in the wrong hands,' Troy said, 'but Dynamo is an expert in these matters, and no one will get hurt.'

Dynamo grinned. 'Let's teach them a lesson they will never forget.'

Troy chuckled. 'You are going to frighten the daylights out of them.'

'Serves them right,' Lucy muttered.

'They are going to pay for what they've done,' Sammy said.

'I hope they die of fright,' Beasley said, swishing his tail.

'Oh, I hope so too,' Foxy said.

They said their goodbyes and left.

BOOM! BANG! WHIZZ!

'It's now or never,' Dynamo whispered. 'We have waited long enough.'

'I will stay and give Dynamo a hand to light the fireworks,' Sammy said.

They knew their voices could be carried on the night air. Trolls could hear a pin drop. So dynamo and Sammy got to work quietly.

The fireworks illuminated the sky.

They exploded one after another in a rainbow of colours that was magical to see.

The trolls had been sitting idly around a fire. They stared up in amazement as the night sky lit up in a display of colour, followed by loud booms and bangs. The fireworks whizzed everywhere.

The trolls had never seen fireworks before. They were terrified and ran in all directions as the fireworks whooshed past them like rockets.

WHOOSH, WHOOSH, WHOOSH, went the fireworks.

BOOM! BOOM! BANG! WHIZZ! BOOM! BANG!

'Now is our chance,' Troy said. 'Come on, Lucy.'

Troy and Lucy raced to the little hut where all the fairy folk were squashed together.

Troy reached up, grabbed the key, and quickly turned it in the lock. Then with Lucy's help, they threw the door open.

Troy stood back and beckoned silently to them to come out after a glance around to see if the coast was clear.

They all ran out.

'Quick! Get on the train!' Troy called urgently.

Lucy gave a helping hand to the weaker ones. A little pixie tripped and fell, and Chico ran over, took her by the hand, and pulled her towards the train.

As soon as they were aboard, Troy jumped into the driver's seat and started the engine. Lucy sat at the back in one of the carriages and checked that they were all there.

'GO! GO! she shouted, glancing over her shoulder.

The trolls were running after them.

The engine chugged into life, and they were off. They went faster and faster until they were racing along, leaving the trolls far behind.

Suddenly there was a terrific explosion.

Troy chuckled. 'Bang on target,' he said. 'Dynamo has done us proud and blown up the mine. BOOM!' he called. 'BOOM! BOOM! BANG!'

All the passengers laughed out loud. They were so happy to be going home.

WE CAN GO HOME NOW

The firework display was over.

'We can go home now,' Sammy said, chuckling.

'I've never enjoyed myself as much as I have tonight,' Dynamo said.

They both laughed together quietly in the darkness.

They untied the ropes to free the balloon, quickly jumped into the basket and floated gently away.

'We did it! We did it!' Dynamo whooped. 'We blew up the mine!'

'We must have a party as soon as we are home,' Sammy said.

'With fireworks.' Dynamo said.

They both howled with laughter.

Dynamo pointed down. 'Look, there's the train.'

'It won't be long before they are home,' Sammy said.

Far below, the train was speeding along. Happy, smiling faces filled the windows like excited children. Then they all saw the balloon and began to wave madly.

'Look! They've seen us.' Sammy laughed and waved down at them.

Dynamo waved and laughed too. 'I can see Troy driving the train, and there's Lucy.'

A gust of wind blew them steadily along, and they faded away into the distance. Finally, they landed safely on the ground.

Troy stopped the train at the station and jumped out, followed by Lucy. They watched as everyone climbed out happily. Chico was helping the little pixie he had saved. But she still seemed scared, as if she couldn't believe she was finally free and on her way home.

A little elf took out his flute and began to play a merry tune, and the music echoed around the hillside.

They sang merrily as they went along.

'Heigh, diddley heigh-ho, it's home we go. Heigh, diddley heigh-ho, it's home we go. Home is the place we love to be, with friends and family. Heigh, diddley heigh-ho…'

The village came into sight.

A loud cheer went up, and they all ran home.

PARTY TIME

The party was in full swing.

A large trestle table full of homemade pasties, daintily made sandwiches, chocolate buns, and jugs of juice sat to one side.

A musician played a jolly tune on his fiddle, and all the fairy folk enjoyed themselves.

'Help yourself,' an elf said and rubbed his hands on his pinny.

'Wow!' Lucy said. 'This looks fantastic.'

Troy helped himself to a plate full of goodies. 'Tuck in,' he said.

'It's good to be home again,' a little elf said to his friend, laughing

They were all so happy the danger was over.

'What if they come back?' an elf said.

'WHAT?' They all stared at him in horror.

A goblin stamped his foot and glared at the little elf. 'What do you want to go and say a thing like that for?'

'They were so angry at us for blowing up their mine they will want revenge,' the elf added grim-faced.

'And we stole their train,' another elf chipped in.

'They can come back whenever they feel like it, and we can't stop them,' someone else cried.

'Well, what are we going to do about it?' fairy Tulip said, shaking with fear.

'They could come back and bash our heads in,' another goblin said.

A grumpy-faced gnome stood. 'We can't live in fear for the rest of our lives,' he said. 'We are all going to be nervous wrecks.'

They were all very upset and frightened.

'There must be something we can do?' Felix the elf said.

A wise little pixie spoke quietly, 'I know what we can do.' They all turned to look at her. 'We must ask the wizard for help.'

'But he lives in a far, far away castle,' an elf said.

'He is the only one who can help us now,' Dobbin the wise said.

They all agreed.

'But who will undertake such a dangerous journey?' they all said together.

'I am the one to go,' Troy said. 'I am the only one who has ever been away from home,' he added.

'I'll go with you,' Lucy said. She had been sitting quietly, listening to the others.

Troy gasped. 'Are you sure you want to come with me? It could be very dangerous.'

Lucy stood up. 'Yes, I am.'

'Very well,' he said, 'but we don't know the way.'

'I know the way,' a gnome said. 'I can fly you there in my helicopter.'

Troy turned to look towards a gnome with spiky red hair. 'Oh, Speedo, that's marvellous,' Troy said.

'I'll meet you at the aerodrome in five minutes,' Speedo said, hurrying away to get things ready.

Chico came running towards them. The little pixie was with him. They had become firm friends and had been playing together.

'Come on, Chico, it's time to leave,' Lucy said excitedly.

Troy looked at the monkey. 'I think Chico wants to tell us something.'

Chico chattered away to Troy as Lucy looked

curiously on.

'He doesn't want any more adventures,' Troy said, smiling with great understanding.

'I see,' Lucy said. 'What shall we do then?'

'Why not take him to monkey paradise where he will be happy,' the pixie said. 'It is a secret place, and I know he will love it there. We can go now.'

'Oh, that sounds wonderful,' Troy said. 'Would you like to go and live there with all the other monkeys, Chico?'

Chico chattered happily away to Troy.

'That's settled then,' he said, turning to Lucy. 'He wants the freedom to live in the woods with the other monkeys.'

'Then he must go there,' Lucy said and looked at Chico. 'I'm going to miss you.'

Chico jumped up and put his little arms around her neck, and she hugged him as they said goodbye.

Troy hugged Chico too. 'You have been a good friend to us,' he said. 'And we are going to miss you. But I have a feeling we will see you again.'

The pixie smiled. 'My name is Popsy, and I want to share some of my magic pixie dust with you. You only have one wish that will come true, so use it wisely.'

She gave Troy a small black velvet pouch, which he tucked away in his jacket pocket. 'Thank you, Popsy', he said, smiling at her. 'Take good care of Chico.'

They said goodbye and hurried away to get ready for the journey.

MARGARET D. CLARK

A MOUNTAIN LION

Speedo stood by his helicopter, ready to leave. 'Come on, there is not a moment to lose,' he shouted as they ran towards him. 'A storm is brewing, and we don't want to be caught. Quick! Get in.' He opened the side door. 'And don't forget to put your seat belts on.'

All the villagers had come to see them off. 'Good luck,' they cried.

Once they were safely inside the helicopter with the door firmly closed, Speedo turned on the controls, and the engine roared into life.

They flew over mountains, rivers, and trees. Then, it went dark, and big black clouds filled the sky. Then, finally, the castle came into view.

Speedo pointed to the castle. 'That is where the wizard lives,' he said and started his descent.

They landed safely on the ground.

'I can't help you anymore,' Speedo yelled over the engine's noise. 'You will have to find your own way back. I can't fly in a storm.'

'We wouldn't want you to,' Troy said. 'You have been a great help and a true friend.'

Lucy smiled. 'You have been marvellous.'

'I like to help my friends out.'

They quickly climbed out. The helicopter was soon up and away.

'I hope he gets home safely,' Lucy said.

'He will be back well before the storm breaks,' Troy replied confidently.

They watched him disappear into the distance, then ran for cover. It was hard going against the wind and rain.

'Quick, head for that cave over there,' Troy said.

They were about to enter when they heard an angry roar.

'YOU ARE NOT WELCOME HERE!'

A huge mountain lion stood at the entrance.

'Please let us in,' Troy said. 'We only want shelter until the storm passes.'

'Oh, very well,' the lion growled. 'As long as you are not moving in.'

Troy frowned. 'We wouldn't dream of it. Are you hurt?' he asked as the lion limped to one side so they could pass.

They quickly entered the cave and were shocked to see how thin he was.

I have a splinter in my paw, which is too painful to walk on. I haven't eaten for ages, and if I stay here, I will die.'

'Oh, dear, you must let me help you,' Troy said.

'Do you think you can?' the lion said. 'I'm too young to die.'

Troy walked over to the lion. 'Let me take a look.'

The lion rolled onto his back like a big kitten, holding his paw out for Troy.

Troy and Lucy inspected his paw intently and saw the huge splinter wedged deeply in his pad.

'That looks nasty,' Troy said.

'Oh, you poor thing,' Lucy said. 'You must be in awful pain.'

'This might hurt a bit,' Troy warned as he took a firm grip on the splinter and pulled it out. 'I have it here in my hand for you to see,' he said, holding it up to show them.

The lion jumped to his feet and gave a mighty roar.

'The pain has gone, and it doesn't hurt a bit. You have saved me from a horrible death. What are your names?'

'I'm Troy, and this is Lucy.'

'And I am known as Lion.'

They smiled at him.

'Now we are friends, may I know what you are doing here? Don't you know how dangerous it is?'

'We have come to ask the wizard for help,' Troy said. 'The trolls could attack my village anytime, and my friends could be in danger,' he added. 'We need a way to stop them from ever coming back.'

'Then I feel sorry for you,' Lion said. 'Horrible creatures, trolls.'

They made themselves comfortable and chatted away like old friends. Then, as soon as it had stopped raining, they went outside into the clear mountain air.

'Goodbye, Lion', they called as they were leaving.

'Goodbye, my friends,' Lion roared.

THE WIZARD'S CASTLE

A mysterious grey mist swirled around the castle, and they decided it was the creepiest thing they had ever seen.

'I wish we didn't have to go in there,' Lucy said.

Troy looked at her. 'We have no choice if we want to save everyone. We must go in,' he said. 'Don't worry, you will be safe with me.'

Lucy rolled her eyes at him as much as to say, 'and what can you do?'

Troy searched for an entrance. 'We must find a way in.' A door suddenly opened. 'Someone knows we are here,' Troy said.

'Yes, they do,' Lucy said, looking around.

'Well, what are we waiting for?' Troy said. 'We can't stand here all day.'

They went straight in.

'Hello,' Troy called, and his voice echoed around the ancient stone walls. 'Is anyone there?'

'Who be a calling?' a voice from inside said.

'We have come to see the wizard,' Troy shouted. 'Is he here?'

The castle was dimly lit, making it difficult to see who was speaking.

'You are talking to him.'

'Please, can you help us?' Lucy said.

'I might, and I might not,' the voice said. The door behind them silently slid shut, trapping them inside the castle. 'And who are you?'

'My name is Troy, and this is Lucy.'

'I am known as Whizzy the wizard, and you are most welcome.'

Then, as if by magic, the inside lit up with a thousand dancing fairy lights making the place look magical, and the wizard stood in front of them.

He was a surprise to them.

His long black cloak was covered in stars. On his head was a big pointy hat, and his long flowing white beard almost reached the floor.

'That surprised you,' he said, beaming. 'All my dear wife's idea. You must come and meet her.' He chuckled. 'She makes an excellent chocolate cake – the best I have ever tasted. Come on. It's this way.'

Doors opened and closed all by themselves as they hurried along. Then, finally, they entered a room full of injured animals. A bald eagle was in one corner with a broken leg. A badger had a bandage around his tummy, and a squirrel had a bandage around his tail. An owl perched in one corner with an eye patch over one eye, and a tiny mouse had a sticking plaster on his nose.

The animals all sat quietly together.

Troy gazed at them. 'Wow. This is fantastic.'

Lucy stared around in wide-eyed wonder.

It was the strangest room they had ever been in.

A fire burned brightly at one end of the room. A young woman with long black hair that reached the floor looked at them with kindly brown eyes as she attended to an eagle with a broken wing.

'This is my dear wife, Arabella,' the wizard said proudly.

She smiled at them in a friendly way. 'Whizzy's

friends are always welcome,' she said. 'I remember the last time we entertained visitors was over a hundred years ago.'

Whizzy raised his eyebrows. 'As long as that? How time flies.' He smiled fondly at her.

'I am finished here,' Arabella said. 'Will you put him back in his nest for me?'

'Of course, I will, my dear.' Whizzy took the eagle from her and placed it gently in a nest high up in one corner, out of reach of the others. He spoke softly to it as he stroked its head. 'Sleep now,' he murmured. The eagle fell under his spell, closed his eyes, and slept.

Lucy and Troy stood silently, watching in wonder at all they saw.

'I expect our visitors are hungry after such a long journey,' Arabella said, getting up. She turned to Lucy and Troy. 'Come with me, my dears.'

She went over to a bare table in the corner of the room, waved her arms over it, and muttered something they didn't understand. And lo and behold, the table was suddenly full of the most delicious food.

Troy and Lucy gasped and looked at each other.

'Why not sit here, my dears? Then we can start.'

'Thank you,' Troy and Lucy said together as they sat at the table.

'Whizzy, be a dear and pour out the juice.'

Whizzy filled a glass with golden-coloured juice for each of them.

They looked curiously at it before taking a sip.

'Ooh, this is wonderful,' Lucy said.

Troy nodded his head in agreement after taking a big drink. 'Sunflower juice,' he added. 'My favourite.'

'Don't be shy. Tuck in,' Arabella said, smiling at

them both.

'I am hungry,' Troy said, who always ate every scrap of food put in front of him

Lucy stared at the chocolate cake. 'That looks amazing.'

They began to eat.

'Wow!' Troy said when he had finished. 'I have never tasted anything so scrumptious in all my born days.'

'Everything tastes delicious,' Lucy said and finished a cream scone.

Once the meal was over, Arabella swished her hands over the table, and everything magically disappeared.

Troy and Lucy gasped in amazement. It was all done so quickly.

Troy grinned. 'No washing up.'

It made them all laugh.

Arabella fixed her eyes on Lucy. 'Your parents are alive and well.'

Lucy stared at her in astonishment.

'My dear Arabella is never wrong,' Whizzy said, smiling. 'Now down to business. How can I help you?'

Troy explained everything to them. 'The trolls can come back anytime,' he added worriedly.

Lucy nodded in agreement.

'How can we stop them?' Troy asked.

'Can you help us?' Lucy said and bit her bottom lip.

'Of course, I can help you,' Whizzy said. 'Come with me.'

They hurried out after him. Arabella stood watching them leave. 'Goodbye, my dears,' she called after them.

They entered a small cave through a secret door and saw a rock pool full of clear water.

'This is the pool of destiny,' Whizzy said. 'All truth lies here.' He began to stare intently into it and said the magic words. A strange mist formed over the pool of destiny, and pictures appeared, but only Whizzy could see them.

Finally, the mist melted away, and the pool became clear again.

Whizzy turned to face them. 'I have the answer to your problem. It's a tropical plant with a spikey blue flower that grows on the hillside in a land far, far away. The trolls will never come near when that is in the ground. So you must plant it and let it grow around the perimeter of your land, and you will be safe forever.'

Troy rubbed his chin. 'Where is this land?'

'You will need help to get there, and I know someone who may assist you,' Whizzy said. "Come this way.' Then, as he turned to leave, he paused briefly to pick up a small bag from the shelf nearby and gave it to Troy. 'Here, take this. You will find what you need inside.'

Troy put it hastily in his pocket. 'Thank you.'

'You must hurry if you want to save your friends.'

Lucy and Troy followed Whizzy until they reached a vast cavern open to the ocean.

Whizzy stood on a narrow ledge with his back to them and gave a piercing whistle. 'We will not have long to wait,' he said. 'My friend is shy and not used to strangers, and we do not want to frighten him. So stay well back and remain quiet.'

Troy and Lucy stood silently at the back of the cave, wondering what would happen next.

THE SEA MONSTER

Troy and Lucy gasped as a huge sea monster popped his head out of the water.

Whizzy spoke quietly to him, 'Hello, my friend. I need to ask a favour.' A strange exchange took place between Whizzy and the sea monster.

'Wow!' Troy said. 'He is amazing.'

Lucy stared wide-eyed. 'Oh, isn't he wonderful.'

The sea monster gave a toothy grin.

'His name is Serpent, and he is a sea horse,' Whizzy said. 'He will take you where you need to be.'

'You mean we get to ride him,' Troy said.

'How else will you get there?' Whizzy replied and gave a toothy grin identical to the sea horse.

Lucy jumped a little when she saw it.

'Climb on,' Whizzy said. 'There is not a moment to lose.'

Serpent waited patiently until they were both seated on his back.

'Good luck, my friends,' Whizzy called out as the sea horse swam away. The tide carried them along as they rode off, up and down, and over huge waves.

Lucy laughed. 'Oh, this is fantastic.'

'It's the ride of a lifetime,' Troy shouted behind her.

They saw land in the distance, and as they drew close to it, they could see a sandy beach surrounded by palm trees.

Serpent swam steadily towards it.

'We are nearly there,' Lucy said, and Troy agreed.

Serpent swam into shallow water so they could paddle ashore, and they climbed down from his back.

'Thank you,' they said.

'You have been a wonderful friend,' Troy shouted.

Serpent gave them the same toothy grin he had before, swam swiftly away and was soon gone.

DRAGON FIRE

Troy and Lucy stepped onto the golden sands. They stopped and looked at each other when they heard a voice.

'What are you doing here?' the voice said. 'Don't you know how dangerous it is?' The voice belonged to a dragon.

Suddenly, the beach came alive with monster-sized crabs. They were heading straight for them.

'Run!' Troy yelled. 'They are going to eat us!'

But there was no escape. The giant flesh-eating crabs crawled everywhere.

Lucy screamed. 'I don't like it here.'

'They want to gobble you up,' the dragon said. 'Here, let me help you.'

The dragon blew a blast of fire that had them scuttling off.

Troy and Lucy stared at him and grinned.

'Wow,' Troy said. 'That was brilliant.'

Lucy smiled. 'Thank you for saving our lives.'

'I rather enjoyed that,' the dragon said. 'Now, if you will excuse me. I must be on my way.'

'Would you mind telling us your name before you go?' Troy asked. 'I like to know who my friends are.'

'I am called Hero,' the dragon said. 'Well, what are you waiting for?'

They quickly ran off the beach to safety and stopped to watch Hero fly off high into the sky.

'He's magnificent,' Troy said. 'Hero saved us from being eaten by the crabs.'

Lucy grimaced. 'Urgh,' she said with a little shiver.

MAGIC FLOWERS

Troy and Lucy began their search as the parrots chirped merrily in the trees.

Troy took two little trowels out of the bag Whizzy had given him.

'Here, you will need this,' he said and gave one to Lucy.

They soon found the plants with the spiky blue flower, just coming into bud and growing wildly on the hillside.

Lucy smiled. 'Don't they look lovely?'

Troy held up the trowel. 'Let's get to work.'

They carefully dug out several small plants and put them away into the little leather bags they had brought.

'We have enough now,' Troy said. He pulled the drawstring to keep them safe from falling out. 'We must plant them in the ground all around the village.'

'There's still plenty left,' Lucy said, gazing happily around.

They turned sharply as they heard thunder in the distance.

'A storm is brewing,' Troy said, looking up as a flash of lightning streaked across the sky.

The rain came lashing down.

''Quick, we must find shelter!' he said.

'Head for the trees,' Lucy cried.

They took shelter beneath the trees as the storm raged and water poured down from the heavens.

Troy frowned. 'We must protect the plants from getting wet,' he said and tucked them neatly inside his jacket to keep them dry.

The storm was soon over.

Lucy peeped out from the trees. 'It's stopped raining,' she said as rainwater trickled down her wet face and hair.

'HELP! HELP!' a voice cried.

Troy looked around. 'Someone is in trouble.'

'It sounds like it's coming from over there,' Lucy said, pointing.

They headed for the swollen river that had burst its banks and saw a head bobbing about in the water. The cries for help were getting weaker. The rapids lay ahead.

Lucy gasped. 'Oh, no, someone is drowning. What are we going to do?'

'We must save him,' Troy said.

They ran alongside the river, desperately wondering what they could do to help him, when they saw an elephant waiting at the bend in the river. He was waving his trunk out over the water and bellowing loudly.

'The elephant is trying to save him,' Troy said.

'Save me! Oh, please save me,' the voice shouted.

'Hold on,' Troy yelled and pointed to a huge log that had come loose in the storm. 'Hold this,' he cried to the elephant, and the massive beast curled his trunk around it. 'Throw it in and make a bridge across the river,' Troy called.

The elephant hurled the big log. It landed across the river, making a bridge.

Lucy watched on from the riverbank. 'Oh, be careful, Troy.'

He began to crawl across the log until he was over the river. Then he lay full length on the log holding out his arms and waited until the boy was close enough to catch.

'Reach up, and I will catch you,' Troy said as the drowning boy was swept towards him.

The boy reached desperately out with his hands flailing wildly. Troy grabbed him and pulled him out of the water. They lay on the log for a moment. The boy gasped and spluttered as Troy held onto him.

The elephant slowly pulled the log back onto dry land.

'You are safe now,' Troy said as he stepped off the log onto the safety of the bank.

The boy gradually stopped spluttering and stood up. 'You have saved my life, and I am grateful to you. My name is Abdu, and this is Samson, my elephant friend.'

'I'm Troy, and this is Lucy, I'm glad I was here to help, but I couldn't have done it without Samson. He did most of the work, and it's him you should thank.'

'He is my friend,' Abdu said and put his arms around Samson's thick trunk and spoke quietly to him.

Troy and Lucy watched in amazement as Abdu and Samson had a conversation. Finally, Abdu drew away and looked at Troy. 'You can speak with elephants?'

Troy nodded. 'Yes, I can.'

'Samson has told me this.'

Lucy smiled at them both. 'You two don't know how lucky you are.'

They both grinned at her.

They watched as the elephant walked away.

THE MAGIC CARPET

Abdu looked at Troy and Lucy. 'Why are you here?'

Troy explained to him what the trolls had done and how Whizzy had told them to pick the plant with the blue flower to stop the trolls from entering the village again. 'They could come back at any time,' Troy cried.

'We must leave at once if we are to save them,' Lucy added.

Abdu glanced over his shoulder. 'It is not safe here,' he said.

As he spoke, a fierce-looking tribe of warriors with painted faces carrying spears ran towards them.

'It's the Booboo tribe!' Abdu cried in horror. 'Quick, we must hide.'

They ran for their lives.

Troy and Lucy followed Abdu into the thick forest and quickly hid in the ruins of an old temple.

'They won't find us here,' Abdu whispered.

Many hours passed before they crept out of their hiding place. Then, all was silent in the forest.

'It's safe to come out now,' Abdu said, looking around.

Troy and Lucy followed Abdu out just as the sun was setting.

'I don't understand,' Troy said, scratching his head.

Lucy frowned. 'Are they always this friendly?'

'I think you had better explain, Abdu, and tell us what is going on,' Troy said frowning.

Abdu puffed out his chest. 'I am Abdu, the explorer,' he said. 'I like to visit strange places. I love all animals, and they seem to like me,' he added with a smile.

Lucy pulled a face. 'You can't love those horrible flesh-eating crabs!'

Abdu shook his head.

Troy narrowed his eyes. 'Why were you not eaten?'

'That is my little secret I hope to share with you in time.' He gave a cheeky grin. 'When I first saw the Booboo tribe, I knew they were dangerous, and I would be taken prisoner if they saw me. I was just about to leave when I fell into the river. You saved my life, and I am grateful to you.'

The drums had started up in the jungle.

'I don't like the sound of that,' Lucy said.

Troy frowned. 'They sound like war drums.'

'Come with me,' Abdu cried. He was off like a rocket, and they raced along beside him.

He took them to a cave-like structure, pulled out a roll of material, and laid it flat on the ground.

Troy gasped. 'A flying carpet.'

Abdu grinned and gestured for them to climb on. 'Hop on,' he said, laughing at the look on their faces.

'You're kidding me,' Lucy said but stepped quickly onto it.

Troy joined her.

'Quick, get down!' Abdu yelled just as a spear flew past them, missing them by inches. 'We are about to be captured, and they will show us no mercy.'

They flattened themselves on the magic carpet as the Booboo tribe ran towards them, their spears held high, ready to throw. They were inches away from being captured when Abdu uttered some magic words, 'Hold on,' he cried as the magic carpet whooshed high up into the air, and they were safely away.

The Booboo tribe stared up at them in astonishment. Troy, Lucy and Abdu couldn't stop laughing at the look on their faces.

'That was a near thing,' Troy said once they were flying gently along high up in a clear sky.

Lucy sat up and looked around her. 'This is amazing!'

'Wow,' Troy said. 'I've always wanted to fly on one of these.'

They sat close together as they flew silently through the night sky with only a silver moon to light the way. The ground was far below as they flew over oceans, rivers and trees.

'This is magical,' Lucy said. 'How do I get one?'

And they all started laughing.

A SAFE LANDING

They headed for a group of dome-shaped buildings. It was night when they finally landed and stepped off the magic carpet.

'I am home now and must leave you here,' Abdu said. 'My mother will be missing me.'

'We are grateful for all you have done,' Troy said.

Lucy grinned. 'You have been a good friend to us.'

Troy nodded. 'The best.'

'You will use magic to take you home,' Abdu said with a wink. He rolled up his carpet and tossed it carelessly over his shoulder. No one would ever know it was a magic carpet.

It was time to take their leave. They said their goodbyes, and Abdu hurried away to disappear into the darkness.

Troy felt around in his coat pocket and brought out a small pouch. 'This will take us to my home,' he explained. 'Popsy gave me some of her pixie magic. It will grant us one wish.'

Lucy clapped her hands. 'Oh, how exciting! I do love magic!'

'You must close your eyes when I say. No peeping, and don't open them until I say you can. I will make the wish to send us home.'

Troy sprinkled them both in pink clouds of pixie magic. 'Close your eyes,' he said softly, and Lucy shut her eyes tight.

'Take us both to Havenlea,' Troy whispered.

In an instant, they had gone.

Lucy felt a strange floating sensation then she

heard Troy's voice. 'You can open your eyes now,' he said. 'We are back.'

She opened her eyes, looked around and gasped. 'As quick as that,' she said with a big grin.

HAVENLEA

Their friends came running out of their homes to greet them as soon as they saw them.

'They are back!' a goblin cried, running towards them.

'Troy and Lucy are back!' a gnome said.

They were quickly surrounded by smiles of hope and anxious looks.

'Have you found the answer to our problem?' a little elf said.

'We have,' Troy said, carefully taking out the plant with a spikey blue flower in bud from his little bag. 'This will solve all our problems and stop the trolls from returning.'

They all stared at the plant. 'But it's only a little flower,' a gnome said.

A goblin threw up his hands. 'What good can that do?'

'Oh, shut up and let him speak,' Popsy said. 'He has risked his life to save us, after all.' Chico clapped his little hands.

A murmur of agreement was heard.

Lucy stepped forward. 'The wizard told us the trolls won't dare come back with this in the ground.'

There was a stunned silence.

'Well, it must be true,' an elf said, followed by murmurs of approval.

Troy opened his bag. 'We have work to do,' he shouted at the top of his voice.

The plants were carefully passed around and quickly planted in neat little rows around their homes.

Everyone was pleased with their work.

Suddenly a voice called out.

'THE TROLLS ARE COMING! THE TROLLS ARE COMING!'

A goblin keeping watch at the edge of the village was yelling at the top of his voice as he came running towards them. 'THE TROLLS ARE COMING! THE TROLLS ARE COMING!' He raced into the village and waved his arms about.

The march of heavy feet could be heard heading towards them.

'Quick hide!' Troy shouted. 'We don't want them to find us here.'

They all scattered and ran back to their homes, locking their doors behind them.

Troy and Lucy ran to shelter in the little brick shed with wide windows that had a good view. They peeped out, hardly daring to breathe.

Everyone watched and waited to see what would happen. They watched the trolls running towards them, each carrying a big club, intent on mischief. They were about to enter the village. Then the most amazing thing happened.

The plants began to glow, and the spikey blue petals on the little flowers opened, sending out a strange smell that filled the air.

The trolls started coughing, sneezing, and running about in all directions, rubbing their noses as the smell invaded their nostrils and made their eyes water. They were bumping into each other and falling over in their haste to escape.

Soon, all the Trolls had gone, and the flowers returned to normal.

Everyone came out of their homes with big smiling faces laughing and chuckling loudly. They had all watched through their windows the strange antics of the Trolls in amused fascination.

'That was the funniest thing I have ever seen,' a goblin said, doubled up with laughter.

An elf chuckled. 'We've seen the last of them. They won't dare come back after this.'

There was happiness all around, and Lucy and Troy were treated like heroes.

Thousands of miles away on an unknown island, a group of marine biologists were about to be rescued. Among them were Lucy's parents.

MARGARET D. CLARK

THE MESSENGER

It was a peaceful time. Troy and Lucy sat quietly together.

Troy glanced up into the cloudless blue sky. 'We have a visitor,' he said wisely.

Lucy saw an eagle flying towards them. 'He looks familiar,' she said, studying him.

'Whizzy has sent us a message.' Troy put out his arm, and the eagle landed right on it.

'Hello, old friend,' Troy said.

A strange conversation took place as Lucy looked on in awe.

Troy turned to Lucy as the eagle flew away. 'Whizzy sent him to tell you the good news. Your parents are safe and well.'

Lucy smiled and jumped in the air. 'I knew they would find them!'

'You never doubted it,' Troy said, grinning widely at her.

Suddenly there was a massive bang. They looked at each other, startled.

'Something's wrong,' Troy said.

They ran to investigate.

They were astonished at what they saw. The balloon had burst with a terrific explosion due to a tree lying across it. Unfortunately, someone had cut it down, and it had fallen in the wrong direction.

'Now look what you've done,' Sammy shouted.

'Oh, dear, oh dear,' the tree cutter said tearfully. 'I've ruined your balloon. Please forgive me, Sammy.'

Sammy stamped his feet. 'Well, what are you going to do about it?' he said as a crowd gathered around.

A pixie looked at the balloon. 'We can fix that, no bother. We can use magic.'

Everyone agreed, and they all circled the balloon and started singing a funny little song.

Sammy smiled as the log rolled off, and the balloon started to blow up again until it was as good as new.

Sammy was delighted, and everyone stopped singing.

'We've never had a ride in it,' a gnome said sadly.

'I would love to ride in that,' said someone longingly.

A pixie pushed through the crowd. 'So would I,' she said.

Sammy turned to them and raised his eyebrows. 'Would you really? Well, what are we waiting for!' he cried. 'Form a queue, and I will take as many as possible.'

Merriment filled the air as everyone formed into a line.

Sammy was delighted that his balloon rides were so popular. And he knew that he would be very busy giving more in the future.

*****

Troy and Lucy sat quietly in the shade of a giant oak tree.

'It's wonderful to see them so happy,' Lucy said as she watched the villagers chatting in little groups.

'They are free at last. And look, Chico is coming to see us.' Troy smiled broadly.

Lucy grinned. 'He hasn't forgotten us, then.'

The little monkey chatted away and threw his arms around Lucy to hug her as if he was saying a final goodbye before scampering off into the trees.

'Why do I get the feeling I won't see him again?' Lucy said as she watched him go. 'What did he say to you, Troy?'

'He said he is delighted living in monkey paradise and has made lots of friends, and he wants us to be happy too.'

They both sat quietly for a moment.

'Is there anything you would like to do now,' Troy said.

Lucy yawned. 'I want to go home.'

'No place like it,' Troy said, but she was already asleep.

'Goodbye, Lucy, you will always be my friend.' He smiled gently at her, then worked his magic, and Lucy disappeared.

CHRISTMAS

The town hall was holding the annual Christmas sale. The stalls were full of people picking up things they wished to buy.

Lucy's mum was busily serving behind the stall counter filled with all sorts of exciting things.

When she saw a little circus outfit for sale, Lucy came over to give her a hand. She recognised it right away. A pair of little red shoes curled up at the toes and a bright yellow outfit that belonged to Troy. She gazed at them as the memory came flooding back. 'Troy,' she murmured to herself.

Two ladies stopped to chat, and Lucy could hear them talking.

'Did you know the orphanage has been closed and boarded up?'

'No, I didn't know. Tell me what happened, Maud?'

'Well,' Maud, the town gossip said, 'somebody had complained to the authorities about the state of the orphanage, so they sent someone round to inspect it, and it was so bad it was closed down the next day.'

'But what happened to all the children?' Ethel said, looking as if she had swallowed a wasp.

'Well,' huffed and puffed Maud, 'they were all adopted into nice families.'

'All of them?'

'Yes, every single one, even the cat.'

'Well, I never!'

'The strange thing is,' Maud paused with a puzzled look. 'What I don't understand is that no one knows who it was that did the complaining.'

The two women moved away, but Lucy had

overheard them talking and knew Troy had kept his promise and made it all happen.

OTHER BOOKS BY THIS AUTHOR

The Magic Kingdom – Chosen as a top read in Kindle direct publishing in UK, USA & Canada.

The Legacy – Also adapted as a stage play.

Printed in Great Britain
by Amazon